SHERLOCK SAM and the MISSING HEIRLOOM in KATONG

SHER
SAM

By
A.J.
LOW

Andrews McMeel Publishing®

a division of Andrews McMeel Universal

Sherlock Sam and the Missing Heirloom in Katong copyright
© 2012, 2016 by Adan Jimenez and Felicia Low-Jimenez. Illustrations copyright © 2012, 2016 by Epigram Books. Illustrations and cover design by drewscape. Original English edition published by Epigram Books Pte. Ltd. All rights reserved. Printed in China. No part of this book may be used or reproduced in any manner whatsoever without written permission except in the case of reprints in the context of reviews.

Epigram Books Pte. Ltd.
1008 Toa Payoh North #03-08 Singapore 318996
Tel: +65 6292 4456 / Fax: +65 6292 4414
enquiry@epigrambooks.sg / www.epigrambooks.sg

Andrews McMeel Publishing
a division of Andrews McMeel Universal
1130 Walnut Street, Kansas City, Missouri 64106

www.andrewsmcmeel.com

16 17 18 19 20 SDB 10 9 8 7 6 5 4 3 2 1

ISBN: 978-1-4494-7789-9

Library of Congress Number: 2015959733

Made by:
Shenzhen Donnelley Printing Company Ltd.
Address and location of manufacturer:
No. 47, Wuhe Nan Road, Bantian Ind. Zone,
Shenzhen China, 518129
1st Printing—5/9/16

ATTENTION SCHOOLS AND BUSINESSES
Andrews McMeel books are available at quantity discounts with bulk purchase for educational, business, or sales promotional use. For information, please e-mail the Andrews McMeel Publishing Special Sales Department: specialsales@amuniversal.com.

For Faith, Jordan, Timmy, and our parents

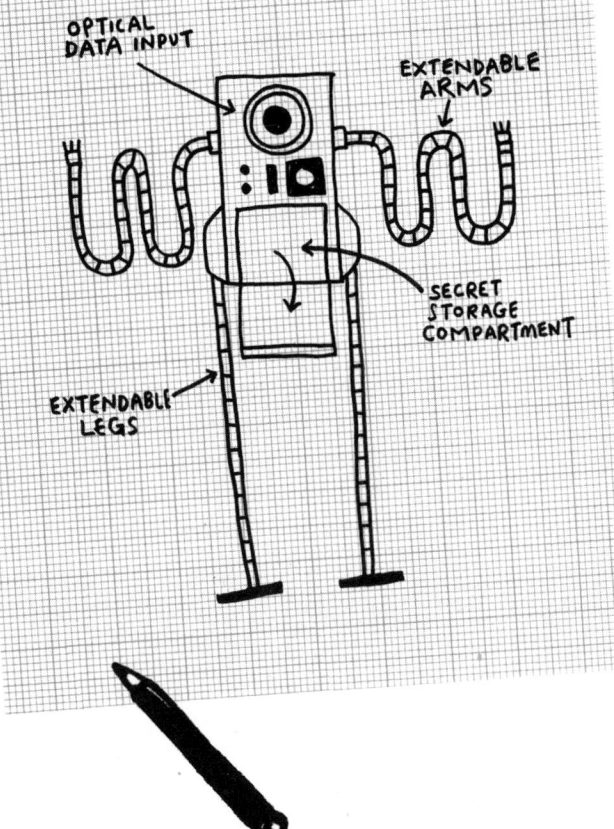

CHAPTER ONE

"Just one final tweak here..."

I put the screwdriver down and sat back to admire my robot. Those trips to the Robotics Learning Laboratories at the Science Centre with Dad sure came in useful! Now, what should I name him?

"Maybe, MEGAMECH! No, no, no. DESTROBOT! No, wait, TECHNODOOM! No, I've got it! MEGA-DESTRO-TECHNO-BOT!"

I flicked the robot's switch.

"What-is-my-name?" the robot said in a mechanical voice as it came to life.

"What, son?" Dad said, popping into my room at exactly the wrong time.

"My-name-is-Wat-son," the robot repeated.

"DAD! What have you done?" I yelled out in horror.

"What, son? Mom said come and eat. Dinner's ready," Dad said.

"Ooh, dinner! Why didn't you say so earlier? C'mon . . . Watson," I said.

I went to the kitchen and Mom was making chicken rice—one of my favorites!

"Can I have the drumstick, please?" I asked.

"Cannot! You're so chubby already!" my big sister, Wendy, said. Wendy is a year older than me and she is the artist in the family. We get along . . . sometimes. Mostly when she needs help with her Chinese homework.

"It's okay. He's a growing boy." Dad and I spend a lot of time together. He's an engineer, and very smart.

"You can take ONE drumstick, but less rice." Mom cooks super delicious food all the time, but never gives me enough. I don't understand why. I'm a growing boy after all.

I am Sherlock Sam. Well, my real name is Samuel Tan Cher Lock. In case you couldn't tell, Sherlock Holmes is one of my heroes, and I want to be a great detective, like him!

"Does the robot need his own plate, Sam?" Mom asked. My family is no longer surprised when my inventions turn up at the dinner table. In fact, some of my earlier creations are used by the family often, like the homing device I created for the TV remote control that Mom is always misplacing.

"My-name-is-Wat-son," Watson replied.

"Watson, would you like to try my chicken rice?" Mom said. Mom stays at home and her job is to take care of all of us. She is a fantastic mom.

"No-thank-you," Watson said. "I-only-eat-batteries."

"His name is Watson? Clever, Sherlock," Wendy snickered.

"Actually, Dad named him," I mumbled, biting into my drumstick.

"I did? Clever me! When did I do that?" Dad asked. Dad is super intelligent, but Mom says he is lost in his own world. One time,

Mom asked him to buy broccoli and he brought back cauliflower. He thought it was unripe broccoli.

"Don't forget we're going to meet Auntie Kim Lian tomorrow, kids," Mom said.

"Can I not go? I always have to look after Cher Lock," Wendy said.

"It's SHER-lock!" I mumbled again, cleaning off my drumstick.

"Sam, what can Watson do?" Dad asked.

"Uh . . . can I tell you later? May I have another drumstick, please?" I didn't want to reveal my master plan in front of Mom.

After we finished dinner, Dad came to my room. He placed a couple of books on my desk.

"So, what didn't you want to say in front of Mom?" he asked.

I walked over to the door to make sure that it was tightly shut before I spoke. I pulled Dad down to sit with me on the floor.

"Watson can extend his arms and legs. To reach farther places than you or I can," I whispered, leaning in close, just to be extra careful.

"Or higher places, right?" Dad whispered back. See? Dad's very smart.

"Yeah, higher places, too."

"Sam, just make sure Mom doesn't catch you." Dad stood up, then turned around. "And if she does," he continued in a whisper, "this conversation never happened." We grinned at each other.

"Right. This conversation never happened," I said. "So, what books did you get me this time, Dad?"

Dad immediately beamed. He loves talking about books, especially treasures that he finds at secondhand bookstores.

"I got you a comic on logic called *Logicomix*!"

"Cool! Does it have maths in it?" I asked.

"Read it and find out," Dad replied, grinning.

"And did you get me that *other* book you promised?" I whispered, turning to check that the door was still closed.

Dad ruffled my hair and tossed me the book.

"Remember, this conversation never happened," he said as he left the room.

I clutched the new Batman comic happily. Too many people think comics are just fun things that kids read, but comics are so much more! Batman is my hero because he uses his deductive abilities and great intelligence to battle crime! He's such a great detective; he even stars in *Detective Comics*!

Later that night, I took Watson for a test run. We snuck into the darkened kitchen. Watson walked over to where Mom kept her secret tin of Khong Guan biscuits high up in the cupboard, and extended his legs. My favorite biscuit was the double-chocolate biscuit—I made sure Watson knew which one to target first.

As he was opening the cupboard, we heard Wendy's door open!

"Watson!" I whispered. "Hide!"

"I-knew-this-would-be-trouble," Watson said.

"Shush!" I grumbled.

I slid under the dining table, and Watson retracted his legs while holding on to the cupboard door.

Wendy walked into the kitchen and went to the refrigerator. Suddenly, she stood up straight. She looked at the cupboard, but

Watson had pulled himself into the cupboard before he could be seen. That was close!

Wendy shrugged and poured herself a cup of water. After her bedroom door closed, I breathed a sigh of relief.

"Watson," I called softly. "Where are you?"

He opened the cupboard door and extended his legs down to the floor. We quickly snuck back to my room.

"Watson, pass me the biscuits, please," I whispered.

"You-have-already-eaten-two-drumsticks. Why-are-you-still-hungry?" Watson questioned.

"Shush!" I replied.

Watson pressed a small button located at his stomach. A secret storage space opened and inside were my favorite double-chocolate biscuits! I didn't tell Dad about the secret compartment. The less he knew, the less Mom could torture out of him. Munching happily on my biscuits, I patted Watson on his metal head. I was starting to like this new invention of mine. We were going to be good buddies, I could tell.

"Do-not-get-crumbs-on-the-bed. I-do-not-want-ants-in-my-circuits," Watson said.

Then again, maybe not.

◦◦◦

CHAPTER TWO

I woke up covered in double-chocolate crumbs.

"Oh no! I hear Mom coming!" I jumped out of bed and started sliding the crumbs under the bed. "Watson, help me!" I said.

I could tell Watson was not a willing accomplice—I had to keep poking him to hurry. It was almost as if he wanted to get me in trouble just so he could say, "I-told-you-so." Before I knew it, Mom was standing at my door.

"Sam, are you ready? It's Saturday! We are having breakfast with Jimmy and Auntie Kim Lian at Chin Mee Chin, remember?"

"Of course I do!" I said, kicking the last crumb beneath the bed. I love eating breakfast at Chin Mee Chin Confectionery. It is my favorite place in Katong, but Mom says I can't go too often.

The little bakery along East Coast Road was very crowded. Jimmy and his grandma, Auntie Kim Lian, were already there and had saved us seats. Auntie Kim Lian is Peranakan, like Mom, and her family has lived in Katong for generations. Jimmy is a friend from class, and I noticed he was holding a library copy of one of my favorite books, *Charlie and the Chocolate Factory*.

Chin Mee Chin is special to Mom because the bakery still looks like it did in the old photographs her family had taken when she was a little girl.

"Hello, Auntie Kim Lian. Hello, Jimmy. I would like two slices of *kaya* toast with extra butter and extra *kaya*, please," I quickly recited. Jimmy's eyes widened when Watson sat down next to him.

"Slow down, Sam, the rest of us haven't decided what we want yet," Mom said.

I was busy analyzing the cream cones lined up neatly in the display case. I immediately noticed that they were not all of the same length and width.

"I would also like one cream cone, the third one in the second row, please," I continued.

"Sam, introduce Watson to Jimmy," Mom nudged.

"Watson, introduce yourself to Jimmy," I said, distracted by the new tray of piping hot cupcakes that had just come from the kitchen.

"Hello-Jimmy. My-name-is-Wat-son," Watson said.

"Wow! I'm Jimmy!" Jimmy replied.

"I'd also like one of the plain butter cupcakes

covered in sprinkles. The fifth one in the third row," I quickly added.

I was trying to decide if I should have a Milo, too, when I heard two nicely dressed ladies next to us talking about a Peranakan restaurant that everyone seemed to be going to recently. I made a mental note to tell Mom to head there for lunch. I really wanted to place our orders before that big cream cone was snapped up!

"Mom!" I said impatiently.

"Yes, Sam?" Mom replied.

"Are we going to order yet?" I asked. I told Mom what I wanted.

"Oh boy, Cher Lock, you're going to make yourself sick," Wendy said.

"Mom! Do you remember what I want?" I poked her, ignoring Wendy.

"Yes, dear. Third one in the second row; fifth one in the third row; two *kaya* toast, extra butter and extra *kaya*; and a cup of Milo." From the expression on Mom's face, I knew I shouldn't bring lunch up yet. Mom called to the shop auntie to place our orders.

Jimmy kept staring at Watson. He looked him over from every angle while Watson stared at the strange little boy who walked circles around him. Then Jimmy poked Watson.

"Please-do-not-poke-me," Watson said.

"You can complain?" Jimmy asked, surprised.

"Of-course. Everyone-can-complain," Watson replied.

"Wow! What else can you do?" Jimmy asked.

"I-am-not-at-liberty-to-discuss-what-I-can-do," Watson said.

I frowned at Watson. Now he had made his abilities sound all mysterious!

"*Aiyoh*, Samuel, you are such a handsome boy," Auntie Kim Lian said, her hands cupping my face and squishing it.

"Gank you Ang-tee," I struggled to reply. I don't understand why people are always squishing my face. Dad says it is because I am handsome. But I would rather be tall than handsome.

"Do you want to come over to Auntie's house later? I am thinking of making your favorite *ayam buah keluak.*"

Of course I did! Auntie Kim Lian's *ayam buah keluak* is legendary! Her chicken is tender, but not too mushy, and her delicious gravy is perfect for pouring all over a plate of warm, fragrant rice. Plus, she never stops me from getting second, or even third, helpings, like Mom does.

But first, I had to make sure that it would be safe. Auntie Kim Lian can be forgetful sometimes.

"Auntie Kim Lian, have you soaked the *buah keluak* long enough? Those nuts can be poisonous if you don't soak them in water for at least a week, you know!" I said.

"Poisonous?!" Jimmy yelled. "My mama would never poison anyone!"

A sudden hush fell over Chin Mee Chin.

Auntie Kim Lian laughed, breaking the tension. "Of course I've soaked them long enough! I've been cooking *ayam buah keluak* since before you were born, Samuel!"

"Auntie Kim Lian has been cooking *ayam buah keluak* since before *I* was born!" Mom said.

Just then, a young man came up to our table.

"Hello, Auntie Kim Lian! Nice to see you here. I wanted to thank you for your help that day! I couldn't have finished my project without your precious family recipe book," he said.

"Oh, hello, dear," Auntie Kim Lian replied, smiling. "It was no problem at all. Your mom is my good friend; of course I will help her son."

"Next time, Auntie will cook for me, right?"

Auntie Kim Lian laughed and agreed. Everyone wanted Auntie Kim Lian to cook for them! But today, she was going to cook for me!

"Mom! Can we go eat *ayam buah keluak*? Please?" I asked hopefully.

"Yes, Auntie!" Jimmy said. "I want Watson to come over and play! Can they come over right now instead of only at dinner?" Watson does not play, I wanted to say, but I decided that Jimmy's reason would only help my cause.

"I don't want to cause you trouble or anything," Mom said.

"No, it's okay," Auntie Kim Lian replied. "I will cook dinner tonight, and you can bring your husband. We'll have a feast!"

"Well . . . when you put it that way, how can I say no? Kids, don't cause Auntie Kim Lian too much trouble! Dad and I will come later," Mom said. "Thank you for the invitation, Auntie Kim Lian. And Wendy, take care of your brother, okay?"

"Every time," Wendy said, exasperated. She then whispered to me, "You owe me help with my Chinese homework for this!"

I shrugged, munching happily on my cream cone.

CHAPTER THREE

With breakfast out of the way, I was ready to focus my full attention on the feast Auntie Kim Lian promised us. Mom asked if Auntie Kim Lian could serve healthy tuna sandwiches for lunch. Tuna wasn't of particular interest to me, not when there was *ayam buah keluak* for dinner!

"Is your *ayam buah keluak* recipe from the precious family recipe book the uncle was talking about, Auntie?" I asked.

Auntie Kim Lian was driving and we were all squished into her car. Wendy was in front, and Jimmy, Watson, and I were huddled in the back.

"Yes it is, Samuel. My family recipe book is so precious to me, I consider it a family heirloom!" Auntie Kim Lian replied.

"Wow," Wendy said. "Has it been in your family for long?"

"Let's see. This recipe book has been in my family for many generations. Even before my grandparents came to Singapore from Malacca," Auntie Kim Lian replied.

"Does that mean that the recipes came from way back then as well?" Wendy asked.

"Yes, dear, from my *Mak Cho*," Auntie Kim Lian said.

"My great-great-great-great-great—wait, how many greats is that?" puzzled Jimmy, staring at his fingers in confusion.

"What's a *Mak Cho*?" Wendy asked.

"It's a great-grandmother," I answered. "Our Mama's mom is our *Mak Cho*."

"My *Mak Cho* started writing her home-cooked recipes when she married my *Kong Cho*. It was very important for Peranakan women to learn to cook well for their husbands back then," Auntie Kim Lian continued.

"Wendy would have made a terrible Peranakan wife back in the olden days," I said.

"Shush, Cher Lock," Wendy shot back.

"It's SHER-lock!" I poked her.

"I would be lost without my family recipe book. And I want to hand it down to my grandchildren and their children," Auntie Kim Lian said as she parked the car. "I've even been teaching Jimmy how to cook *ayam buah keluak*!"

We had arrived at her two-story bungalow with a big garden.

"Girls! Gina! We're home! We've brought friends!" Auntie Kim Lian said.

"How many sisters do you have, Jimmy?" I whispered.

"Four!" Jimmy replied. "Auntie Gina is our family helper."

I made a face. One sister was bad enough. I could not imagine living with four!

Auntie Gina came up and handed Auntie Kim Lian a letter, which she squinted at until Auntie Gina passed Auntie Kim Lian her reading glasses.

"Mam, you forgot to bring your glasses out again," Auntie Gina said.

"I'm so forgetful nowadays, Gina. You must look after me, okay? I can't read anything without my reading glasses," Auntie Kim Lian said, laughing. She put the letter down on a nearby table.

Just then, I saw four girls running toward us. I took cover behind Auntie Kim Lian. Four sisters! Amazing!

"What did you get us? Did you get cream

cones? I want *kaya* toast!" they all shouted at once.

Auntie Kim Lian laughed and called them each by name to come and take their goodies from Jimmy.

Based on height and level of bossiness, I deduced that the oldest was Rose, the second oldest was Martha, next was Donna, and the youngest was Amy.

The girls grabbed their snacks and went to the kitchen.

"Auntie, are you going to start cooking now?" I asked innocently.

"Yes, dear. As soon as I take out my recipe book. I don't cook *ayam buah keluak* very often because good *buah keluak* is hard to find. I've forgotten some of the steps. Auntie is old already, you know," Auntie Kim Lian said, smiling.

I followed Auntie Kim Lian into her enormous kitchen, where Jimmy's sisters were eating their snacks, and she went to a drawer to take her cookbook out. I was amazed to see that she had two fridges! I wondered if one was especially for desserts.

Auntie Kim Lian suddenly called out, "Gina! I can't find my recipe book! Is it in the living room?"

Auntie Gina appeared in the kitchen in a flash. Watson, Jimmy, and Wendy trailed in after her.

"No, Mam. You always keep your recipe book in that drawer," Auntie Gina replied.

"It isn't there. Where could it be?" Auntie Kim Lian asked, puzzled.

"It's okay, Mama! I copied the *ayam buah keluak* recipe out, remember? You said the best way to learn it was to write it out! So I wrote it out!"

Jimmy dashed out of the kitchen.

"That still doesn't tell me where my book is, though," Auntie Kim Lian said. She and Auntie Gina were opening and closing all the

25

cabinets and drawers in the kitchen looking for the book. "It has to be here somewhere! How am I going to cook dinner? We have guests!"

I knew I had to step in because I could see that Auntie Kim Lian was getting more and more worried! Plus, the longer it took to find Auntie Kim Lian's precious family heirloom, the later dinner would be!

"Let's retrace your steps, Auntie. When was the last time you had the recipe book?" I asked.

One of the first rules of detective work is to start from the very beginning. People often forget important details that seem small to them. It's my job to find out what they are.

"Did I use it to make curry yesterday?" Auntie Kim Lian asked Auntie Gina.

"No, Mam. I asked you how you remembered the recipe and you said it was like riding a bicycle," Auntie Gina said.

"Sherlock-should-ride-a-bicycle-before-dinner," Watson said.

While glaring at my robot, I suddenly recalled something.

"Could you have loaned it to that uncle we met at Chin Mee Chin, Auntie? He said he couldn't have finished his project without your precious family recipe book," I said.

"Oh, that's right! I did bring it out that day. When was that, Gina?" Auntie Kim Lian asked.

"I think it was two weeks ago, Mam. You haven't used it since," Auntie Gina replied.

It is also important to be very specific about details.

"Think really hard, Auntie Gina. Which day was it?" I said.

"It was . . . a Sunday!" Auntie Gina said.

"How could I forget? I brought it to Katong Antique House that day! The young man was going to photograph it along with other Peranakan family heirlooms for his project," Auntie Kim Lian said.

"Could you have left it there?" I asked.

"I might have. I was distracted talking to my friends. Oh, how careless of me!" Auntie Kim Lian said.

"But if they found Auntie's book, wouldn't they have called her?" Wendy asked.

"I've been there once with Mom and it's filled with old Peranakan things. Maybe they just didn't realize what it was," I said, confident in my theory.

Just then, Jimmy ran back into the kitchen waving a crumpled piece of paper in the air.

"I found it, Mama! I found it! Here's your *ayam buah keluak* recipe!" he said.

Auntie Kim Lian took the piece of paper from him and squinted at it carefully. She then adjusted her glasses and held the paper farther away from her face, but that didn't help at all. After readjusting her glasses one more time, she gave up.

"Thank you, *sayang*. But your handwriting is

so messy, Mama cannot read it even with her reading glasses on!"

Jimmy took the paper and squinted at it as well.

"It's not neat?" he asked.

Wendy looked over Jimmy's shoulder and her eyes widened.

"Those are actual words?!" she said in shock.

Amy, Jimmy's youngest sister, began eyeing Watson with wonder.

"I-am-Wat-son. What-is-your-name?" Watson said, extending his hand out to Amy.

Amy's eyes widened.

"Um . . . my name is Amy. Uh . . . would you like some of my cupcake?"

"No-thank-you. I-would-like-some-batteries-please. I-need-to-recharge-if-we-are-to-search-for-the-missing-heirloom."

"Wait here, I'll go find some!" Jimmy said, before zipping away.

Suddenly, Wendy shouted, "Is that a hamster?"

She pointed to a cage in the backyard.

"That's Benjamin, our hamster," Amy said.

"He's so cute!" Wendy ran to the cage. Benjamin was a brown hamster with white spots. He was running on his wheel.

"I found them! I found them!" Jimmy shouted. He was running so fast, he almost ran over me. Proudly, he handed Watson a couple of batteries.

Watson looked at them and said, "These-have-no-power-left. They-are-perfect. I-can-recycle-them-for-power. I-not-only-look-good-I-am-also-good-for-the-environment."

Jimmy was ooh-ing and ah-ing at Watson. And Wendy was ooh-ing and ah-ing at Benjamin, the hamster.

I felt it was my duty to bring the conversation back to what was important—finding Auntie Kim Lian's precious family heirloom and eating *ayam buah keluak* for dinner! I had also realized exactly where Katong Antique House was located and what that meant . . . another trip to the nearly next door Chin Mee Chin!

"Well, let's go to Katong Antique House and look for your recipe book there. Come on, Watson, Wendy, Jimmy!" I said. Everyone ran after me, except Watson and Auntie Kim Lian. I practically had to shove Watson into the car. I couldn't understand why he wasn't more excited at the chance to solve a mystery!

"*Aiyoh*, slow down, Samuel! Auntie is too old to run!" Auntie Kim Lian said, smiling.

"And Auntie Kim Lian," I said, as I finished stuffing Watson into the car and shutting the door, "maybe we could go back to Chin Mee Chin to pick up another cream cone?"

Auntie Kim Lian laughed, which I took to mean yes.

ooo

CHAPTER FOUR

"What did you say, Samuel? Why did I do what?" Auntie Kim Lian asked.

I was munching on the delicious cream cone I had just bought from Chin Mee Chin. My mouth was stuffed full and it was difficult to talk, but time was of the essence and I couldn't spare an extra moment to chew properly! I looked up to see Auntie Kim Lian, Jimmy, and Wendy looking at me, trying to puzzle out my meaning.

GULP. I tried to brush the crumbs off my

T-shirt as innocently as I could.

"Please-do-not-get-crumbs-in-my-circuits-again," Watson said.

"I think my brother wanted to know why you brought your recipe book out if it's so precious to you?" Wendy said.

"Did you understand him, too?" Jimmy whispered to Watson.

"He-often-talks-with-his-mouth-full," Watson said.

"Well, I think it's very important to preserve our Peranakan heritage," Auntie Kim Lian replied.

"So they wanted you to cook for them, right, Mama?" Jimmy said, nodding wisely.

"No, *sayang*, the young man wanted to take photographs of Peranakan heirlooms from different families. I thought I'd bring the recipe book to Katong Antique House so he could finish his shoot in a day," Auntie Kim Lian gently corrected.

When we reached Katong Antique House, I could still smell the *kaya* toast from Chin Mee Chin. The melting butter smelled like bacon! Focus, Sherlock! I told myself.

I looked at Katong Antique House. It is a beige shophouse with traditional Peranakan designs below the windows on either side of the front door. There are also two Chinese lanterns hanging from the ceiling, in front of the door.

"What does your recipe book look like, Auntie Kim Lian? Is it big and grand? With designs, drawings, and pictures?" Wendy asked, as we entered Katong Antique House.

"Oh, it is a big, thick book! We stuffed it so full with photographs and notes, all handwritten, you can't even close it properly anymore," Auntie Kim Lian said.

"Wow, it must be worth a lot of money!" Wendy replied.

"No, I don't think so. It is so old, the pages

are turning yellow. And there are *belachan* stains on the front cover! The photographer wanted to take photos of the recipes, but I said no. I only allowed him to photograph the book's front and back covers. Our family recipes are for family only," Auntie Kim Lian continued.

"But Mama, then how do you teach the Peranakan cooking class at the community club?" Jimmy asked.

"Well, *sayang*, I never teach recipes from our family book. I only teach from library books I borrow," Auntie Kim Lian replied.

When we walked in, two elderly ladies

greeted Auntie Kim Lian and they immediately started chatting. Like any good detective, I quickly observed my surroundings. The room was slightly cramped and musky. There were lots and lots of Peranakan artifacts around. One cupboard was filled with old cutlery and patterned bowls and plates. Another had clothing of various sorts for men and women. In one corner, there was a plaque with a picture of a bunch of people, whom I deduced to be important Peranakans. There was also a table of Nonya *kueh* right in the middle. A simple white box with a card on it was next to the Nonya *kueh*. I wandered over closer.

"Do you remember when I met that young photographer here two weeks ago to have photographs taken of my family's recipe book?" Auntie Kim Lian asked.

"Sure, Kim Lian, you wouldn't even let us touch the book!" one of the aunties laughed teasingly.

"Did I leave the book behind?" Auntie Kim Lian asked hopefully.

"No, no. If you did, we would surely have called you. We know you *jaga* your family's secret recipes with your life," the other auntie said, smiling.

I instructed everyone to look around carefully, to make sure that Auntie Kim Lian's family heirloom wasn't hidden among the rest of the Peranakan antiques. Jimmy tried to balance antique teacups on Watson's head, much to everyone's horror.

"I think Jimmy and antiques don't mix well," I said, as I gingerly put the fragile teacups back where they belonged. Auntie Kim Lian told him in no uncertain terms to stay still and not to touch anything.

"Jimmy-and-robots-do-not-mix-well-either," Watson said.

"Wow, Wendy, that's really pretty," Jimmy said, looking over Wendy's shoulder. Wendy had pulled out her sketch book, and was using a few colored pencils to draw a brightly colored blouse hanging from one of the cupboards.

"What is that pattern on the blouse, Auntie?" Wendy asked.

"Ah, that is a phoenix design. It is one of the most complicated embroidery designs for a *kebaya* blouse," Auntie Kim Lian said.

"You have to wear it with a traditional *sarong*, right?" Wendy continued.

"Yes, dear. I brought your mom to buy a set last time. Next time we'll buy one for you," Auntie Kim Lian replied.

"Er, no. It's okay. It's pretty, but I hate skirts!" Wendy said, causing all the aunties to laugh.

"Can you put dinosaurs on it?" Jimmy asked. "I love dinosaurs!"

"Well, I don't think anybody ever has before, but I don't see why not," Auntie Kim Lian replied. "It's not a traditional pattern, but all traditions start somewhere. Maybe we can make a *batik* shirt for you with dinosaurs on it, *sayang*."

Jimmy grinned widely. "We should get a *batik* shirt for Watson, too! His can have cool robots on it!"

"Sherlock-did-not-give-me-clothing," Watson said.

"Why would you need clothing? You're a robot!" I said.

"Clothing-on-robots-is-cool. Robots-on-clothing-is-cooler," Watson replied.

Discussing robots and robotics is always fascinating but wasn't relevant at this time, especially with the deadline of dinner looming. Plus, I could tell that Auntie Kim Lian was growing more anxious. She kept looking around the room, even searching places that we had already checked.

"Auntie, you said that you teach a Peranakan cooking class? I think you might have left your cookbook there," I said.

"Mama doesn't use recipes from our family cookbook for her cooking class! She said so already!" Jimmy reminded me.

"But I believe she did. Maybe just one time. And I think that recipe was for *kueh lapis*. Correct, Auntie?" I asked.

"Why . . . I completely forgot! How did you know that, Samuel?" Auntie Kim Lian looked surprised.

"Because the cake box over here has a card that says, 'Especially for the best mother in the world! I learned to bake this secret recipe from Auntie K.L.'s cooking class,'" I said, reading the card aloud. "Given your reputation as a fantastic cook, it was easy to deduce that K.L. stood for Kim Lian!"

"Oh! That's from my daughter," one of the aunties said. "She knows I love cakes but she only knows how to bake Western cakes—like chocolate fudge—that I don't like. I was so surprised when she showed up this morning with a box of *kueh lapis*! She said she needed two weeks to get the cake right. I wanted to tell you, but I forgot. Old already *lah*, Kim Lian. She attends your cooking class at the community club."

"She specially requested to learn this. I didn't know she was your daughter!" Auntie Kim Lian said. "I told them that I couldn't remember the recipe and that it was in my family recipe book. I promised I would bring it to the next lesson. How could I forget?"

"But, Mama, you said our family recipes are top secret!" Jimmy said, looking confused.

"Well, *sayang*, making *kueh lapis* is a complicated process and I couldn't remember the exact steps, so after the photo-taking at Katong Antique House, I brought my book to my cooking class," Auntie Kim Lian said. "But I didn't reveal my secret ingredient to my class. That is for every cook to discover on his or her own. I teach them the basics, and I hope that everyone will be able to create their own family recipes. Nothing is better than the dishes you create on your own."

"Where exactly is your Peranakan cooking class, Auntie?" I asked.

"It's at Marine Parade Community Club, Samuel," Auntie Kim Lian replied. "Oh, I do hope it's there. *Ayam buah keluak* takes so long to prepare! We don't have much time!"

Marine Parade Community Club is on Marine Parade Road, right next to Marine

Parade Library. This is a five-minute drive from Katong, where Katong Antique House is.

"Then that's where we're going next!" I said. "Come on, everybody! Back to the car!"

I ran out, but then quickly ran back in. "Maybe we can get some Nonya *kueh* for the ride over?"

The aunties laughed, which I took to mean yes.

◦◦◦

CHAPTER FIVE

"This place smells of delicious food!" I said.

We had just opened the door to Auntie Kim Lian's cooking classroom. We stood at the doorway and surveyed the large room, which had multiple cooking stations. Each station had a portable stove and a mini-oven. At the front of the class was a large table, which was the teacher's table.

"What are all of you doing here?" a voice suddenly said from behind us.

"Ahh!" Jimmy cried, causing all of us to jump. The book that he was holding tumbled onto the floor.

"Oh, I'm sorry! I didn't mean to scare you," a young lady said.

"Jane! It's you! You gave us all a shock!" Auntie Kim Lian said.

"I saw you heading here with children and a robot when I was coming out of the library. I was curious," Jane said.

"This is my grandson, Jimmy, and his two school friends, Samuel and Wendy. The robot belongs to Samuel," Auntie Kim Lian replied, gesturing in my direction.

"So cute," Jane said, pinching my cheeks, ignoring Watson completely.

"How's your *chap chye* coming along, Jane?" Auntie Kim Lian asked.

"Terrible! I'm always over-stewing or under-stewing it," Jane replied. "I also think I may be putting in too much cabbage."

"We'll go through it again tomorrow, okay?" Auntie Kim Lian said.

"Cabbage makes me fart sometimes," I said to no one in particular.

"That's not the only thing that makes you fart," Wendy replied.

"I-have-a-list-of-all-the-things-that-have-made-you-fart-since-yesterday," Watson said.

Wendy snickered.

"Watson, please help me look around the rest of the room," I said. "Quietly."

"Robots-are-always-stealthy," Watson replied.

Auntie Kim Lian went to the teacher's table to check the drawers, but her recipe book was nowhere to be found.

"Oh dear, it isn't here, either! I honestly don't know where I could have left it," Auntie Kim Lian said, looking more and more worried. "If I had known it was not safely at home all this time, I would have gone through these drawers last week."

"Don't worry, Auntie. I'll find it," I replied. I didn't want to see Auntie Kim Lian so upset.

I decided to investigate Auntie Kim Lian's teacher's table again for clues. I opened a drawer and found a transparent ring folder with what looked like an attendance sheet for Auntie Kim Lian's class.

"Auntie, is this the attendance sheet for your class?" I asked, waving the file in the air.

"Yes, dear, it is," Auntie Kim Lian replied.

Watson, Wendy, and Jimmy started to make their way toward me. We looked at the attendance sheet together. Everyone had written down his or her name, telephone number, and email address in the allocated rows. Each row listed in sequence the dishes the class would be learning every week: *otah*, *chap chye*, *kueh pie tee*, *popiah*, *ikan gerang asam*, *kueh lapis*, *babi pongteh*, and *itek tim* this week. The difficulty was certainly ramping up!

Just then, I noticed that Jimmy had picked up

a piece of paper from the floor and was going to throw it away in the nearby trash can.

"Jimmy! What's that you're holding?" I asked.

"This? Nothing important! I'm going to throw it away. You shouldn't litter, you know," Jimmy said.

Not important? Unlikely!

Wendy and Jimmy crowded around me to look at the piece of paper. Watson stood in front of one of the students' work stations and appeared to be in conversation with an electric mixer.

"Wow, this person's handwriting is even worse than yours, Jimmy," Wendy said.

"My handwriting isn't that bad!" Jimmy said, slightly offended.

"It appears to be a recipe," I said, squinting.

"It's for *bakwan kepeting*," Wendy said. "I recognize some of the ingredients."

"You can cook?" Jimmy asked.

"Mom has taught me a few things here and there," Wendy said, with a self-satisfied look.

"I bet you even I wouldn't eat your cooking," I said.

Wendy slapped my head from behind.

"Ouch! Watson, ATTACK!" I commanded, pointing at my big sister.

"You-have-not-installed-any-attack-programs-in-me," Watson said. I made a note to change that as soon as I got back home.

Auntie Kim Lian and Jane were talking about someone who had left the class, so I walked over to where Watson was.

"Did the electric mixer tell you anything important, Watson?" I asked.

"Nothing-important. Her-head-was-spinning," Watson replied.

I wondered if I could install a better humor program in Watson as well. But back to the case at hand!

It was curious. If Auntie Kim Lian didn't leave it at Katong Antique House, or at her cooking class, there had to be somewhere else she went. And then something clicked in my head.

"Jimmy, did you check out that copy of *Charlie and the Chocolate Factory*?" I asked, remembering I had seen Jimmy holding a library copy of the book at Chin Mee Chin.

"No, Mama checked it out for me!" Jimmy replied cheerfully.

"How long ago?" I asked.

"Two weeks ago!" Jimmy said.

I knew it! Auntie Kim Lian and Jane were still talking but I was anxious to solve the case!

"It's a shame," Auntie Kim Lian said to Jane. "She wasn't very good, but it seemed like she really wanted to learn."

"Sorry to interrupt you, Auntie, but I have another question," I said.

"Oh, that's okay," Jane replied. "I should get going anyway. I'll see you in class tomorrow!" Jane left and Auntie Kim Lian turned to me after she waved good-bye.

"You went to the library after your class that Sunday, didn't you?" I asked.

"That's . . . right! Why, Samuel, how did you know that?" Auntie Kim Lian asked, amazed.

I was right!

"I went to the cookbook section," Auntie Kim Lian continued. "I wanted to see if there were any new Peranakan cookbooks that I could borrow and use in my class."

Auntie Kim Lian had already said that she didn't use her family recipes for her class, except for that one time with the *kueh lapis*. Therefore, she had to have gotten the recipes from somewhere.

"I think we should go to the library," I said.

"I want to go to the library, too! I've finished my book! Why do you have to go? Do you want to borrow a book? Do we have homework?" Jimmy asked. He had been making a paper airplane from the sheet of paper with scribbles on it. "What's the homework on? I don't like maths but English is pretty fun."

I was stunned.

"How could you not love maths, Jimmy?" I asked incredulously. "It's the language of beauty! Take pi, for instance. At first glance, it seems a ridiculous, awkward number that goes on forever and ever! But it's that infinity that makes it so fantastic! It helps us perfectly describe a circle in all its various forms, from as small as a coin to as big as the universe!"

Complete silence greeted my excitement.

"There-is-a-67-percent-chance-that-eating-homework-will-make-you-fart," Watson said finally. He was inspecting two spatulas. "The-percentage-increases-if-your-homework-contains-pie."

"Not that kind of pie! Arrgh. Never mind, can we please just go to the library?" I said, exasperated.

"Only if Watson can give us more statistics about your farting," Wendy snickered. "They're definitely more fun than your statistics on maths."

"Enough about farting," I said. "You're all so childish."

All the humans laughed, including Auntie Kim Lian. Not being able to find Auntie's recipe book was really getting to me! In fact, all unsolved mysteries really get to me!

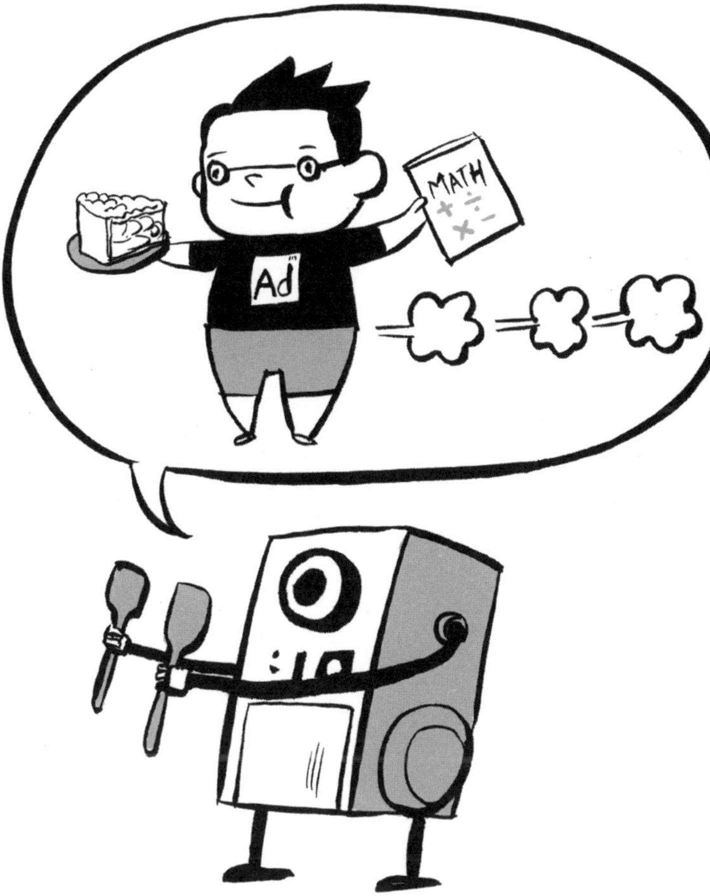
MATH
Ad

"Go check the library for me," Auntie Kim Lian said. "I'll tidy up a bit here and meet you there later."

"To the library!" I shouted.

ooo

CHAPTER SIX

"You guys *wheeze* go ahead. *cough* I'll *grunt* catch up," I said.

Wendy had insisted that we take the stairs even though it meant a three-story climb to the cookbook section of the library.

"The exercise will be good for you, Cher Lock!" she said, smirking at me.

"It's *wheeze* SHER *cough* LOCK! *grunt*," I said, panting. When we reached the top of the staircase, I was so tired, I was ready to fall down.

"Comics!" Jimmy said.

Co-*wheeze*-mics! But first, air!

"Ooh! The art section is up here, too!" Wendy said.

Once I had caught my breath, I quickly walked over to the cookbook section.

"There-are-no-Peranakan-cookbooks-here," Watson said.

"That's weird," I said. "Watson, quickly find out what happened to all the Peranakan cookbooks."

"I-always-obey," Watson said, moving extremely slowly toward the computer. He even typed slowly.

"You could have done that yourself, you know. Faster, too," Wendy said.

"Yeah, I forgot Watson couldn't access the Wi-Fi," I said. "I need to fix that." And have a word with Watson about what *quickly* means.

Watson finally came back from the library computer. "All-the-Peranakan-cookbooks-have-been-checked-out," he said.

"All of them?" I asked. "Someone really wants to learn how to cook Peranakan food. Maybe Auntie Kim Lian accidentally left her recipe book here, and the person who checked out all the books took hers, too."

"It's possible, but how would we know for sure?" Wendy said.

"Let's ask a librarian!" Jimmy said. "This is an emergency!"

We ran back downstairs and noticed there was nobody at the help desk.

"Okay, you guys keep watch," I said. "I'll go see who checked out all these cookbooks."

"Won't you get in trouble, Sherlock?" Jimmy asked.

"Not if you guys keep watch I won't," I said.

I suspected that librarians were not allowed to tell us who checked out books, but I was sure I could figure it out myself. I sat down at one of the terminals and typed in the title of a Peranakan cookbook: *Irene's Peranakan Recipes*. As I typed in other Peranakan cookbook titles, I was surprised.

"Curious," I muttered to myself. Suddenly, Jimmy sounded the alarm!

"Alert! Alert! Library auntie!" Jimmy whispered frantically.

I snuck a peek over the counter and saw that a librarian was coming. I had no time to run back outside without being seen, so I quickly hid under the desk.

"Can I help you?" the librarian asked Jimmy, Wendy, and Watson, who seemed to be standing in a perfectly straight row, blocking her computer terminal from her view.

"Has anybody returned a cookbook, or found one in the library, in the past two weeks? We're looking for a book that doesn't belong to the library," Wendy asked her.

"Not that I know of," she said. "Did you lose your own personal book?"

"No, my Mama did," Jimmy said. "It's her special air-broom!"

"Heirloom," Watson corrected.

"Oh dear. Let me take a look for you in the lost and found, just in case," the librarian said.

"Thank you," Wendy said.

Good thinking, Wendy! The librarian headed toward the back office, and I quickly darted back out.

"Whew!" Jimmy said. "That was close!"

"What did you find out?" Wendy asked.

"Something very strange! The cookbooks have all been checked out by the same person! I saw the person's library card number—it was the same card number each time. But I wasn't able to see the person's name," I said.

Just then, Auntie Kim Lian appeared, while the librarian returned from the back office.

"I'm sorry," the librarian said. "All I found were jackets and sweaters. And one strangely colored sock. But no books. Good luck finding your book!"

Auntie Kim Lian came to meet us. "Did you find anything upstairs?" she asked.

"No, nothing," Wendy said.

"But we found out that all the Peranakan cookbooks have been checked out by the same person, Auntie," I said.

"And how do you know that?" she asked.

"That's not important," I said quickly. "What is important is that I think whoever checked out all those books may also have taken your book, not realizing it wasn't a library book."

"That can't be right," Auntie Kim Lian said. "When I was here two weeks ago, all the Peranakan cookbooks had already been checked out."

That was another theory out the window! Where was this book? Had I missed something important?

"Was there anywhere else you went that night, Auntie?" I asked, eager for another avenue of investigation.

"No. After the library, I went straight home," Auntie Kim Lian said.

Nothing but dead ends so far. Surely this mystery could not vex someone with my detective abilities!

"Maybe it's been in your house this whole time?" I said hopefully.

"Gina and I have looked all over the kitchen, but perhaps we should check the rest of the house," Auntie Kim Lian said. "You kids can look when we get home. Maybe Gina and I missed something in the kitchen, too."

When we got back into the car, Jimmy whispered, "She doesn't show it, but I know Mama is really sad about losing this book. We have to find it, Sherlock!"

"We will," I said. This was a mystery I was determined to solve.

CHAPTER SEVEN

"Watson, if you were a cookbook, where would you hide?" I asked.

After a quick lunch, Auntie Kim Lian went to put little Amy down for her nap. The rest of us made plans to search the house for the missing family heirloom.

"I-am-not-a-cookbook," Watson replied.

"Yes, but if you were—" I continued.

"BENJAMIN IS MISSING! BENJAMIN IS MISSING!" Jimmy yelled, bursting into the living room.

"Oh no! Your cute little hamster is missing?" Wendy asked.

"I went to take him out so that you could play with him but . . . he's escaped!" Jimmy cried, clutching his head and jumping up and down in agitation.

"Don't worry, Jimmy. Watson and I will find Benjamin," I said.

"He must be terrified!" Jimmy yelled, frantically tossing cushions about.

At that moment, Auntie Gina came into the living room.

"Why are you messing up the living room, Jimmy? I just tidied it!" Auntie Gina scolded, clucking her tongue.

"Benjamin is missing, Auntie Gina!" Jimmy cried before running off.

"Again?" Auntie Gina said, shaking her head. She moved around the living room, setting the cushions straight.

"Again?" I said.

"Yes, poor Benjamin goes missing about once a week," Auntie Gina said, smiling slightly.

"What do you do about it?" I asked.

"We leave a trail of hamster food leading back to his cage. He usually follows the trail, then crawls back in to sleep," Auntie Gina replied.

"Hey! That sounds like how Mom gets Cher Lock to do his chores!" Wendy said, smirking.

I glared at Wendy but I could not deny the truth. I also do not understand why I repeatedly fall for Mom's devious trick. Surely I am smarter than that!

"Jimmy!" I called out. Jimmy came scampering back into the room.

"Tell me exactly what happened, and when you discovered that Benjamin was missing," I said.

"Well, I went to his cage and he wasn't there, so he's missing! Benjamin is missing! He's missing, Sherlock!" Jimmy cried.

"Calm down, Jimmy. Let's organize a search party," I said. Someone had to be the adult here. "Wendy, look under the cupboards. Watson, look under the couches. Auntie Gina, show me where the kitchen is."

"I think Watson should search the kitchen," Wendy said, staring at me hard.

No one ever said my big sister was not smart.

"I-will-try-not-to-step-on-any-escaped-hamsters," Watson replied.

"Fine," I said with a huff. "I'll take the couches."

We looked high and low, with Jimmy frantically running about telling everyone not to step on Benjamin. He screamed when Watson stepped on a wad of tissue paper that he thought was Benjamin. We also took the chance to look for Auntie Kim Lian's cookbook.

Wendy found dust balls and I found more wads of tissue paper, but no hamster. Watson even used his powers, secretly of course, to look in the high cupboards in the kitchen, but no Benjamin. Where on earth could that hamster be?

"Jimmy, when did you first discover Benjamin's cage door was open?" I questioned.

"His what?" Jimmy replied.

"His cage door—when did you realize it was open? Or when was the last time you opened his cage door?" I said.

"His cage door wasn't open," Jimmy said.

"What? I thought you said he was missing?" I replied.

"He is! Benjamin is missing! Let's look in my bedroom!" Jimmy cried, almost running off but I caught his T-shirt.

"Jimmy, if the cage door wasn't open, how did Benjamin get out?" I asked.

"He closed it behind him!" Jimmy shouted. "Benjamin is a very polite hamster, Sherlock. He never bites me when I feed him!"

I stared at Jimmy in disbelief.

"To the hamster cage!" I yelled.

We all trooped to the hamster cage in the backyard. I stooped down and looked in the cage. It was filled with hamster bedding, and mounds and mounds of shredded tissue everywhere. But Jimmy was right. There was no sight of Benjamin.

"See! He's not in his cage!" Jimmy said.

"Wait a minute. Auntie Gina, may I please have some broccoli?" I asked.

"That-will-make-you-fart," Watson said.

"It's not for me!" I snapped.

Auntie Gina came back with a piece of broccoli. I broke off a small piece and knelt down next to the hamster cage.

"What are you doing, Sherlock?" Jimmy asked.

"Shush," I whispered.

I opened the cage door and stuck my hand in, gently waving the piece of broccoli about. Sure enough, the large mound of shredded tissue started to quiver and a small little nose peeked out.

"Benjamin!" Jimmy cried.

The hamster sleepily crawled out from his hiding place to nibble at the broccoli. I dropped the broccoli and carefully shut the door.

"I told you not to put in so much tissue paper, Jimmy," Auntie Gina said.

I remembered reading about Occam's razor in one of the comic books Dad got me. It states that the simplest solution is usually the correct one. When Jimmy said that the cage door was not open, I immediately had two theories:

(1) that Benjamin had learned to close the cage door by himself, as Jimmy said; or,

(2) that he had never left the cage in the first place.

One theory was simpler than the other, though when Auntie Gina mentioned Benjamin's multiple escapes, I couldn't just dismiss Benjamin learning how to close doors on his own. He certainly seemed to have had the chance to practice doing that many times before.

"Oh thank you so much, Sherlock! You've solved the Case of the Missing Hamster!" Jimmy shouted.

"That-was-not-much-of-a-case," Watson said.

"Well, we should get back to your grandma's missing cookbook. Shall we head up to your room, Jimmy?" I said, ignoring my robot. A solved case is a solved case, and all mysteries need solving, regardless of how big or small they are!

◦◦◦

CHAPTER EIGHT

"Let's recap," I said, pacing around the room. I had seen Dad do this many times when he was thinking. I was not sure why it helped, but if Dad did it, I would do it as well.

"It wasn't at Katong Antique House," Wendy said.

"It wasn't at Marine Parade Community Club," Jimmy said.

"It-was-not-at-the-library," Watson said.

"And it's not in the house," I said. "We've

double-checked."

"And we know it's not in Benjamin's cage," Jimmy said. "Maybe . . . aliens took it?!"

"No, they would have left traces of faster-than-light travel," I replied. I had read that in a time-travel comic book Dad had borrowed for me from the library.

"Perhaps Benjamin ate it," Wendy said.

"Benjamin wouldn't eat Mama's book!" Jimmy said, offended.

"Watson, please pass me my book," I asked.

"I-live-to-serve," Watson said.

Watson opened his secret compartment and took my copy of *Logicomix* out. Dad knew it would be useful to me because it was about maths and logic. Excellent tools for a detective!

"It doesn't make any sense," Wendy said. "We've searched everywhere and it's not anywhere."

"Which stands to reason that it must have

been taken from Auntie Kim Lian," I said, flipping through my book. "Occam's razor!"

"Oh-come-what?" Jimmy asked.

"Who would want to steal anything from Auntie Kim Lian?" Wendy asked.

"I don't know yet," I replied. "But logically, this is the only conclusion that we can reasonably come to."

"You know, Jimmy," Wendy said, "once we find your grandma's cookbook, you should help her type all her recipes out and print multiple copies for safekeeping."

"I could, sure," Jimmy said, "but Mama loves the book, too, more than the recipes!"

"That makes sense," I said. "It does have the handwritings of her mom, grandma, and great-grandma."

"Plus all the pictures," Wendy said. "You're right. It's a very important family heirloom. But when we find it, you should make copies anyway. Maybe scan the images and the handwritten pages, just in case."

I didn't want to tell her, but that was a very good idea.

Just then, we heard a car pull up outside.

"I think that's Mom and Dad," Wendy said.

"That would be my deduction as well, Wendy," I replied.

We all made our way down to the living room.

"Hey, Mom! Hey, Dad!" I said.

77

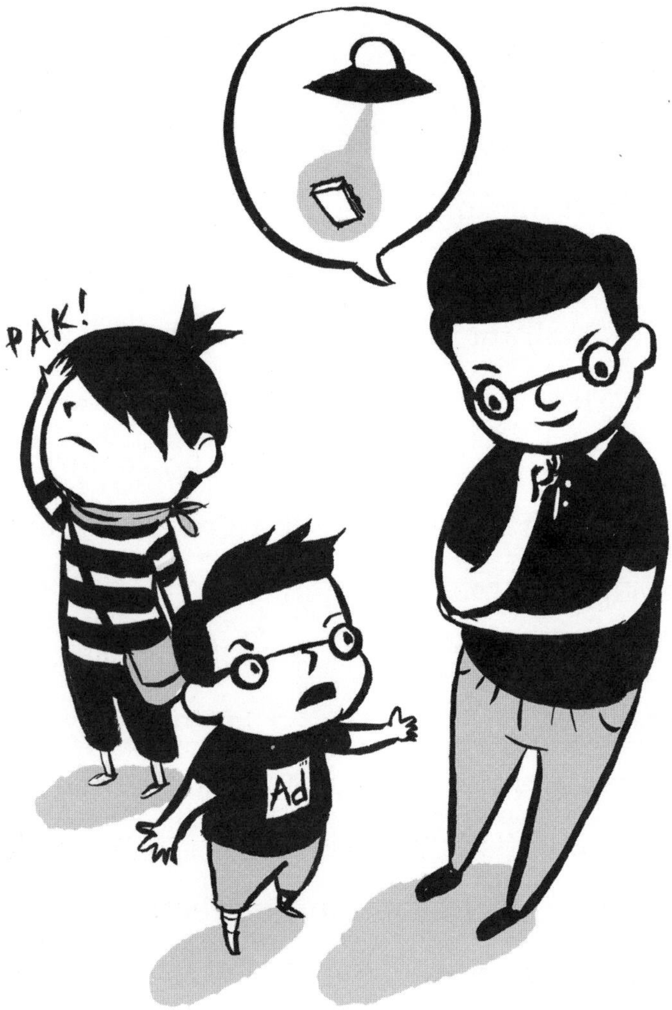
PAK!
Ad

"Hello, Sam. Auntie called and said you were on a case!" Dad replied. We beamed at each other.

"Have the children been behaving themselves, Auntie?" Mom asked.

"Oh yes, yes. They have been very helpful but we still haven't found my cookbook," Auntie Kim Lian replied.

"Have you tried looking for disturbances in the space-time continuum, son?" Dad asked.

I could not see her but I could feel Wendy rolling her eyes.

"Yes, Dad, no disturbances in the space-time continuum, and no traces of faster-than-light travel, either," I replied.

"I see you've covered your bases then, Sherlock," Dad said, nodding sagely.

"I'm very sorry for not being able to cook anything tonight," Auntie Kim Lian said. "I know Samuel was especially looking forward to it."

"Don't worry about it, Auntie," Mom said. "How about we buy you and the children dinner to take your mind off things? Samuel and Watson can look again tomorrow."

"You mean Sherlock and Watson, Mom," I said.

"Yes, dear, I think you meant Sherlock and Watson," Dad repeated, grinning at me.

Mom ignored both of us. Mom and Wendy were quite alike in some ways.

"I've recently been hearing great things about this Peranakan restaurant," Mom said.

"No, no, no, we never eat Peranakan food that isn't home-cooked," Jimmy said, frowning. "Right, Mama?"

"Right, *sayang*," Auntie Kim Lian said, smiling.

"But, Auntie, you know the owner, I think. Her name is Angie?" Mom asked.

"Angie Lim? Is her daughter Marie-Anne?" Auntie Kim Lian said.

"I think so, yes," Mom replied.

"Marie-Anne attended my cooking class at the community club, but she hasn't been to lessons in two weeks," Auntie Kim Lian said. "I suppose I could try her food to show support."

Suddenly, everything clicked into place.

"To the restaurant!" I cried.

"Well," Auntie Kim Lian said, startled, "I guess we better go, then!"

Auntie Kim Lian wouldn't regret it because I was just about to find her missing heirloom!

ooo

CHAPTER NINE

Mom and Dad drove us to the restaurant, with Jimmy squeezed in the back with Watson, Wendy, and me. Auntie Kim Lian was driving her own car, with Jimmy's sisters and Auntie Gina.

We arrived at the restaurant, the New Peranakan Place. It had taken over three shophouses on Joo Chiat Road and painted them all red. It was a two-story restaurant, but even with all the space, there was an enormous line of people outside, waiting to get in.

Thinking ahead like I always did, I'd had Mom call to make a reservation before we left the house, so we had no problems getting a table.

I looked at the menu and saw a lot of traditional Peranakan dishes: *bakwan kepeting, chap chye, popiah,* and many, many more, including my favorite, *ayam buah keluak.*

"Mom, can I go to the restroom?" I said.

"But, Samuel, you haven't ordered anything yet," Mom said, a little worried.

"Just order a small bowl of *ayam buah keluak* for me," I said, getting out of my chair. "Let's go, Watson!"

"That's all you want to eat?" Mom asked, now definitely worried.

"Oh, don't worry," I said, walking away. "I'll be eating a lot more before the night is done."

I felt bad saying I was going to the restroom, but I needed to maintain stealth for this mission. Plus, if I was captured behind enemy lines, Mom and Dad could disavow all knowledge of my actions, because they actually didn't know!

I dragged Watson to the kitchen and we hid under one of the cooking stations. They looked similar to the ones in Auntie Kim Lian's classroom, but were much fancier, and with a lot more food and utensils on top.

There were a lot of cooks and waiters scurrying around, so Watson and I had to stay very quiet and still. I scanned the area and saw a brown-haired woman in a black shirt and slacks. She was holding Auntie Kim Lian's recipe book!

"I knew it, Watson!" I whispered. "It all makes sense now!"

"I-am-sure-you-will-explain-it-to-me-later," Watson said.

"I will, but first we need to get that book back," I said. "No one will believe us without proof!"

We needed to get closer, but with so many people around, how could we do it?

Watson suddenly extended one of his arms and tripped a waiter on our right. He fell with a mighty crash! The woman put Auntie Kim Lian's recipe book down and went to the waiter's rescue, along with everybody else in the kitchen.

"Please-run-across-now-and-make-sure-you-do-not-fall-down-noisily," Watson said, and we ran two stations closer to the book.

"Watson, it wasn't nice to trip the waiter!"

I whispered, turning to check that the waiter was not too badly hurt.

"I-did-not-have-a-choice. It-was-the-only-way-to-do-this." Watson extended his arms across the two cooking stations and picked up Auntie Kim Lian's cookbook. He then retracted his arms and brought it back.

"Good job, Watson!" I whispered. "But that still wasn't very nice. You could have hurt him."

"I-calculated-the-proper-path-so-that-nobody-would-be-hurt," Watson said.

"Well, I guess that's okay," I said. "Quick! We should get out of here before we're noticed!"

I carefully hid the cookbook in Watson's secret compartment before we ran out of the kitchen. Watson and I went to the restroom and I washed my hands because I knew Mom would ask me to do that anyway.

We went back to the table. "Samuel, did you wash your hands?" Mom asked.

"Of course, Mom," I said.

Our food came and we ate quickly. Auntie Kim Lian seemed surprised by everything she ate, and I knew why, even if she never mentioned it.

Once the meal was over, the waiter came over to give us the bill.

"Can I pay my compliments to the owner?" I asked. "The food was very delicious."

"Sure," the waiter said. He was the same one Watson had tripped, but he was perfectly okay.

"Samuel, don't bother the owner," Mom said. "She's very busy, I'm sure."

"Trust me, Mom," I said. "You'll want me to thank them for this meal."

Angie Lim came from the kitchen, looking exactly as she had when I had seen her holding Auntie Kim Lian's cookbook.

"Hi, I heard there was a cute little boy here who wanted to compliment my restaurant," Mrs. Lim said.

"Not quite," I replied. "I actually wanted to compliment Auntie Kim Lian here."

Mrs. Lim's smile faded immediately. "Kim Lian? My daughter's cooking teacher?"

"Oh, she's mentioned me?" Auntie Kim Lian asked. "How thoughtful of her."

"But Auntie Kim Lian, wasn't her daughter the student who stopped coming to your class two weeks ago?" I asked. "You and Auntie Jane were talking about a student that had dropped out, and from the attendance sheet, I noticed that Marie-Anne had been absent for the past two weeks."

"Yes, you're right. Why did Marie-Anne stop coming?" Auntie Kim Lian asked Mrs. Lim.

Mrs. Lim stammered a bit.

"It's okay, Mrs. Lim, we'll answer that question later," I said. "Jimmy found a very interesting piece of paper in the classroom, didn't you, Jimmy?"

"The paper with the horrible handwriting!" Jimmy said, nodding.

"And Wendy realized that it was a recipe for *bakwan kepeting*, isn't that right, Wendy?"

"Yes . . . where are you going with this, Sam?" Wendy asked. She looked worriedly at Mom and Dad.

"Auntie, which student recently asked you about a *bakwan kepeting* recipe?" I asked.

"Why, it was . . . Marie-Anne, I believe. She came up to me after class two weeks ago. But, Samuel, I don't see what this has to do with my missing recipe book."

"And everyone in your class knows you need your reading glasses to read recipes, correct, Auntie Kim Lian?"

"Of course! I'm blind as a bat without my reading glasses," Auntie Kim Lian replied.

"But even with your reading glasses, you still had trouble reading Marie-Anne's handwritten *bakwan kepeting* recipe, didn't you? I also noticed from your notes in the attendance sheet that it was a dish you weren't even teaching in your class."

"Why, yes! The handwriting was . . . not neat," Auntie Kim Lian said.

"That was done on purpose!" I said. "Marie-Anne's handwriting on the attendance sheet was incredibly neat! I deduced that she deliberately wrote the recipe messily as she knew you would have trouble reading her handwriting. And while you were distracted, she stole your family heirloom from your bag!"

"You have no proof of this! How dare you—" Mrs. Lim said.

"Mom," I said, not letting Mrs. Lim interrupt, "you said you heard good things about this restaurant only recently. How long ago is 'recently'?"

"Slightly more than a week ago, actually," Mom said. She looked at Mrs. Lim strangely. "Actually, before that, this restaurant was getting somewhat bad reviews."

"You're absolutely right, Mom," I said. "In fact, you weren't the only one who noticed this. There have been a lot of people talking about the New Peranakan Place, and its recent turnaround. I even heard about it this morning at Chin Mee Chin."

Mrs. Lim was looking very nervous at that point.

"How many Peranakan cookbooks has your daughter checked out from the library, Mrs. Lim?" I asked.

"As many as she could," Mrs. Lim replied. "She was trying to learn, after all. There's nothing wrong with that."

"Yes, but she's had those books for more than a month, and it didn't help your restaurant at all," I said. "No, something happened much more recently. Perhaps two weeks ago, in fact."

Everybody was looking at me, waiting. This was the best part—the grand reveal!

"Might the reason the New Peranakan Place is suddenly doing so well have something to do with . . ." I pushed a button to reveal Watson's secret compartment where the book was hidden. Watson pulled it out, slowly.

Impatiently, I grabbed the book from Watson and shouted, "This!"

I made another note to myself to explain to Watson the need for a dramatic reveal.

Auntie Kim Lian gasped. "My recipe book! Oh, Sherlock, where did you find it?" she asked, reaching out to take her book from me.

"I found it in their kitchen, Auntie," I said. "That's why all the food tonight tasted so familiar to you. They stole your recipes!"

"Mrs. Lim, how could you do such a thing?" Dad said, standing up. "You should be ashamed of yourself!"

"Her restaurant was failing," I continued. "She was desperate to save it."

"That's still no reason to steal from my Mama!" Jimmy yelled.

"When Marie-Anne found out that Auntie Kim Lian would be bringing her family recipe book to class for the first time two weeks ago, she hatched an elaborate plan to steal it. She and her mom then plotted to use the secret recipes. They assumed that Auntie Kim Lian would never find out because she never ate Peranakan food that wasn't homemade. The perfect crime, or so they thought!" I continued.

"And my daughter and I would have gotten away with it, too, if it wasn't for you *kaypoh* kids!" Mrs. Lim said.

"I don't want to do anything drastic, like call the police," Auntie Kim Lian said. "But you must stop using my recipes, or else I will have no other choice."

"Fine," Mrs. Lim said. "We'll stop using all your recipes."

Dad paid the bill, even though Mrs. Lim

didn't deserve the money, and we all got up to leave.

"If Marie-Anne still wants to learn how to cook Peranakan food, she's welcome to attend my classes. I will still be happy to teach her," Auntie Kim Lian said, as she left the restaurant.

I thought that was a really nice thing for Auntie Kim Lian to say.

"Samuel, you did a very nice thing for Auntie Kim Lian," Mom said.

"Don't you mean Sherlock, dear?" Dad asked.

Mom smiled and kissed my forehead. "Yes, I do mean Sherlock."

I grinned. "Well, I didn't do it by myself. Watson and Jimmy helped a lot."

I looked down at my shoes, and then at my sister. "And even Wendy helped."

Wendy smiled. "You did good . . . Sherlock."

"Oh, Samuel, thank you so much. Auntie is so happy!" Auntie Kim Lian said.

"I'm really happy for you, too, Auntie!" I said.

"Sherlock is Singapore's Greatest Kid Detective!" Jimmy shouted.

"Only-when-he-is-hungry," Watson replied.

"Now how about some of that famous *ayam buah keluak*!" I said, ignoring them.

Everybody laughed, so I took that to mean yes.

* * *

A few weeks later, after many delicious bowls of *ayam buah keluak* that Auntie Kim Lian was cooking for me almost daily, Dad came to my room.

"Guess what, son?" he asked.

"What-are-the-guessing-guidelines?" Watson asked.

"He was talking to me, Watson," I said.

I was trying to figure out how to add an attack program into Watson so Wendy would stop coming into my room unannounced.

Unfortunately, there was no way for me to get any military-grade glue traps. Yet.

"The New Peranakan Place has closed down," Dad said. "Without Auntie Kim Lian's recipes to help them, they went back to serving not-so-great food, and nobody wanted to eat there anymore."

"Marie-Anne never went back for any of Auntie Kim Lian's classes, did she?" I said.

"I guess not, son," Dad replied.

"They shouldn't have stolen Auntie Kim Lian's recipe book. I'm sure if they had just asked, she would have helped them," I said.

"You did a very good thing, Sherlock," Dad said. "And I'm very proud of you."

"Thanks, Dad," I said. "I learned everything I know from the best dad in the world."

THE END

GLOSSARY

Aiyoh—Singaporean slang that can mean "oh dear."

Ayam buah keluak—A chicken dish stewed with spices and buah keluak.

Babi pongteh—A braised pork dish with fermented soya bean gravy.

Bakwan kepeting—Pork and crab/shrimp meatballs served in a clear broth.

Batik—Traditional Javanese design made from dyeing cloth. This cloth is often used by Peranakans for shirts and sarongs.

Belachan—Shrimp paste mixed with chiles, minced garlic, shallot paste, and sugar, and then fried. Used in a lot of Peranakan cooking.

Biscuit—Cookie.

Buah keluak—Seeds from the tall trees of the mangrove swamps. The seeds contain hydrogen cyanide and are deadly poisonous if eaten before being washed, boiled, and buried in ash, banana leaves, and earth for at least forty days, and then soaked for four or five days. Once detoxified, the seeds are a mainstay of Peranakan cuisine.

Chap chye—Mixed vegetable stew.

Charlie and the Chocolate Factory—A 1964 children's book by Roald Dahl. The story is about the adventures of Charlie Bucket inside the chocolate factory of eccentric candy maker Willy Wonka. It has been made into two movies.

Chin Mee Chin Confectionery—A well-known old-fashioned bakery located in Katong. Famous for its traditional pastries, cakes, and kaya toast.

Detective Comics—A long-running comic book that has starred Batman since 1938.

Ikan gerang asam—Tenggiri fish, also known as Spanish mackerel, cooked in aromatic tangy gravy with fresh ginger bud, candlenut, fresh chiles, and okra.

Itek tim—A soup containing duck, tomatoes, salted vegetables, and preserved sour plums, simmered gently together.

Jaga—Malay word for "guard."

Katong Antique House—A two-story shophouse located in Katong that holds various Peranakan artifacts and clothing. Owned and curated by Mr. Peter Wee.

Kaya—Coconut jam.

Kaypoh—Nosy or meddling. A busybody.

Kebaya—Traditional dress of a Peranakan woman consisting of a translucent, embroidered blouse and a batik sarong.

Khong Guan—A classic Singaporean biscuit brand, famous for its cream crackers and cream sandwich biscuits.

Kong Cho—Great-grandfather.

Kueh lapis—A cake consisting of thin layers made of butter, eggs, and sugar, piled on top of one another. Each layer is laid down and baked separately, making the creation of a kueh lapis an extremely difficult and time-consuming process.

Kueh pie tee—A thin and crispy pastry tart shell filled with a spicy, sweet mixture of thinly sliced vegetables and prawns.

Lah—Singaporean slang often used to end a sentence and to add emphasis. For example, "Cannot, lah!"

Logicomix—A graphic novel about the foundational quest in mathematics, set between the late 19th century and present day. It is narrated by noted philosopher Bertrand Russell.

Mak Cho—Great-grandmother.

Mama—Grandmother.

Milo—A chocolate and malt drink that is popular with kids in Singapore.

Nonya kueh—Peranakan cakes and desserts.

Occam's razor—A principle of logic that can be simplified into the statement: "The simplest solution is often the correct one."

Otah—Spicy fish cake grilled in a banana leaf wrapping; sometimes also spelled "otak."

Peranakan—Straits Chinese. Descendants of Chinese settlers who settled in Malacca, Penang, and Singapore. Peranakan culture is a hybrid culture incorporating Chinese and Malay influences.

Pi—A mathematical constant that is usually denoted by the symbol π and equals approximately 3.1415. When the circumference of a circle is divided by its radius, it will always equal pi, no matter the size of the circle.

Popiah—A soft, thin paper-like crepe or pancake made from wheat flour that is filled with a variety of ingredients: turnips, bean sprouts, lettuce leaves, grated carrots, slices of Chinese sausage, thinly sliced fried tofu, chopped peanuts, fried shallots, shredded omelette, shrimp, and/or crab meat.

Sarong—A traditional wraparound skirt.

Sayang—An affectionate term meaning "dear" or "sweetheart" in Malay.

ABOUT THE CHARACTERS

SAMUEL TAN CHER LOCK a.k.a. SHERLOCK SAM

A ten-year-old boy with eyes bigger than his tummy. Sherlock's heroes are Sherlock Holmes, Batman, and his dad. Extremely smart and observant, Sherlock often takes it upon himself to solve any and all mysteries—big or small. He loves comics and superheroes!

WATSON

Built by Sherlock to be his trusty, cheery sidekick, Watson is, instead, a "grumpy old man" who is reluctantly drawn into Sherlock's adventures, or, as Watson perceives them, his misadventures. Watson is environmentally friendly.

WENDY

Sherlock's older sister. A year older than Sherlock, Wendy is a very talented artist, but she is terrible at Chinese. Sherlock would like to be taller than her one day soon. She doesn't like wearing dresses or skirts.

JIMMY

Sherlock's classmate, Jimmy is the only boy in a Peranakan family with four sisters. He seems much younger than his actual age, because everything is exciting and magical to Jimmy. He has terrible handwriting.

DAD

An engineer, Sherlock's dad is a scientific genius, but is rather forgetful and bumbling in real life. He has never stopped reading superhero comics—a love he's passed on to his son.

MOM

A homemaker, Sherlock's mom is half-Peranakan and is constantly experimenting in the kitchen. Sherlock often wonders why she tempts him with food, then does not allow him to eat his fill.

AUNTIE KIM LIAN

A Peranakan matriarch, Auntie Kim Lian is renowned for her cooking skills. Fiercely protective of her grandchildren and her family recipes, she loves cooking for Sherlock Sam because he loves her food!

ABOUT THE AUTHORS

The writers behind the pseudonym A. J. Low are the husband-and-wife team Adan Jimenez and Felicia Low-Jimenez. Born in the San Joaquin Valley in California to Mexican immigrant parents, Adan became an immigrant himself when he moved to Singapore after completing his degree in English literature at New York University. He has worked in the book industry and the gaming industry, and has co-written a children's book, *Twisted Journeys #22: Hero City*, published in the U.S. in 2012.

Felicia was born and raised in Singapore. She started work in the book industry after completing her degree in business administration. She also attained her graduate degree in literary theory from the University of New England in New South Wales, Australia. The *Sherlock Sam* series is Felicia's debut writing effort, after accumulating years of experience buying, selling, and marketing books. You can email the authors at sherlock.sam.sg@gmail.com.

ABOUT THE ILLUSTRATOR

Andrew Tan (also known as drewscape) is a full-time freelance illustrator from Singapore. His work consists of drawing storyboards and illustrating for advertising agencies as well as magazines. He enjoys creating comics just for the fun of it. He loves experimenting with various styles and mediums, hunting for new art tools, and discovering new graphic novels with fresh, interesting drawing styles. His inspirations come from daily life, manga, European comics, and science fiction.